Independence

Mine Disaster

By T. L. Shively

Copyright

Published in the United States by Sanhedralite Editing and Publishing
(https://www.facebook.com/DolbyEditingAndPublishing/)

Edited by: Sherrie Dolby
(dolbyduranduran@yahoo.com)

Cover design by: Karima Creations

Acknowledgements

I am thankful for all the support I have had with all my writing. My husband, family, and friends have been the greatest, and I am thankful for them all. But for this book, there are two that I would like to thank above all others:

Douglas Pierce and Brian K. Morris.

Doug and Brian have both been wonderful friends during this past year when I have been dealing with a lot of issues. They have both been awesome sounding boards and both have given me some great advice. Along with that great advice, Doug has also helped me get my Guardians back so that I may continue with their story. Thank you, guys! You both are awesome!

Claw was walking through the halls of the Command Center, his destination that of Czaar's Cantina and Serdita's Brew. Here in Sanctuary, mythics went about their lives in the town of Thetis. The Command Center was the defense forces of Sanctuary, all manned by humans, mostly ones who were descendants of the original Arions, residents of the original Sanctuary that was first founded in Greece.

Six factions made up the Command Center forces; his was the Gamma faction. They were the crystal technicians; no one knew crystals like they did. Every faction had their own specialty, but Gamma was the best, at least to him.

He nodded to those he passed in the hallway, well most, some he smirked at. He knew the names that were whispered behind his back.

Unstable.

Abrasive.

Uncontrollable.

He wasn't sure which his favorite was.

But what no one could argue with was that he was the best when it came to the crystals that the Arions depended on, whether it was for defense, offense, or just to keep the Sanctuary working. It was something that had been handed down throughout his family line and, he knew, the only reason they still were part of Sanctuary.

He could probably work to try to change their opinions of him, but why? He liked that everyone was nervous around him; it kept them from bothering him. He learned long ago what happened when you let your guard down. He refused to make that mistake again.

He had just reached the waterfall exit when he heard the whispering.

"That's him? I thought you said he was intimidating and volatile? He looks just like-"

He had turned and started towards the direction of the healers that were whispering none too quietly off to the side. The one that was speaking was Jake, the newest member to the healers, and who was now frowning at Travis who was slashing his throat trying to tell him to be quiet.

"What?"

Jake jumped when Claw stepped up to them, and his face went white.

"Volatile dinnae mean deaf," he told the now shaking healer who was staring up at him wide-eyed. He looked over at Travis with a brow raised. "Hope ye dinnae plan tae send this one out into the field anytime soon. He will piss his pants the first shadow attack."

With that said he turned around and moved through the waterfall exit hearing

Jake over the sounds of the water falling behind him.

"Told you to watch what you said about him. What part of unstable didn't you get?"

He grinned as he walked over the grassy hills into the forest. He wasn't sure if it was just his Scottish accent or just the fact that he had no problem confronting anyone that had everyone so intimidated by him. Nor did he really care. It was his frankness that was one of the many reasons he never saw eye-to-eye with Ira. That and Claw actually had a mind of his own.

Everyone thought him callous and abrasive all because he wasn't afraid to say it like he saw it and call someone out. Since when did everyone become such a wuss that standing up for oneself was suddenly unacceptable behavior? He would rather be ostracized for being him than be liked for being a door mat.

He didn't get it sometimes.

Just like the big deal with the fabled Guardians that are supposedly going to come and save the day. He snorted at that. There had been six different comings of the Guardians that were known and yet the shadows still come. Supposedly, they stop the biggest and badest shadow of all from destroying life as everyone knows it: The Shadow Magine.

There were many in Sanctuary who didn't believe in the Guardians and then there were the "true believers that thought the sun rose and set with these heroes that still hadn't made an appearance.

Many placed secret bets on whether they believed the Guardians were real or not. He knew the history books spoke of them and how they would come to Sanctuary with powers that no Arion could ever hope to achieve; powers for one thing only: to destroy the Magine.

If only they could find their own way to protect themselves without having to depend on some fictional beings that one never knew when they would show up. If they would show up.

"Claw!"

He nodded to Roy, his gnome pal that was already setting the table up for them. The table was always ready for them whenever Claw walked in, with hand paddles waiting. He walked up to the bar and nodded to Daphne as she poured him and Roy their usual.

Guess it was kind of ironic, him calling the Guardians fictional when he was getting ready to play a game of rainbow ball with a gnome. Then again, he could see gnomes and fairies anytime he wanted. The Guardians, on the other hand, he didn't know of anyone who had physically seen them, unless it was the caretaker Lucius. They say the Gods no longer walk amongst men, but there were times when he watched

Lucius, and he wondered. Could Lucius be a God? If so, he wouldn't let his secret out; he had too much respect for the man.

"Table is ready for us man," Roy hollered to him as he fitted his hand paddle, which was crafted specifically for his stubby little hand.

Roy. What a name for a gnome. Not that he had much room to talk, and he didn't mean Claw. He was very fond of that name. No, it was his birth name that made him shudder in revulsion. He never forgave his parents for that ill-fated joke.

He owed the lass that gave him that moniker, even if it was meant as an insult. One man's trash is another's treasure as they say.

He ambled from the bar to the table. Setting his mug down on a nearby table, he fitted his hand paddle. The amount of stories he had heard regarding his name could fill a novel. Too bad they were complete fiction, although some gave him amusement. His favorite was that he lost his left hand to a shark in a fight to the death, and they had to give him a prosthetic hand. But, of course, he had to wear a claw till they finished the hand.

"Something funny?" Roy frowned at him, but Claw just shrugged and took his turn.

It was a good thing he had acquired the nickname before coming here. Lucius was the only one to know his true name, and that man had enough of his own secrets that he had no problem keeping Claw's. He almost told another, almost. But almost only counted in horse shoes and hand grenades.

Another shot, and the game was almost over, with him being the winner, of course. He never lost a game of Rainbow Ball and didn't plan on starting now. He would love to find the idiot who named the game Rainbow Ball; it required skill, and they gave it a name that befits a toddler game.

When the last of Roy's balls disappeared, he grinned one of his Scottish grins and lifted his mug in a toast.

****

The sounds of whirling and zings from all his creations in his room usually soothed him but for some reason lately Claw had been having issues sleeping. He thought about seeing the head healer, but he truly hated admitting he needed help.

Besides, it wasn't anything medical that was keeping him from sleeping. It was purely analytical. Turning his head, he looked over at the picture of his ancestor, the one who created S.A.M.: Shadow Apprehension Movement. She was the only one in his family who didn't have bright red hair and green eyes but in everything else she was just as brilliant as the rest of them.

Looking at her journal that was lying on the night stand by his bed, he would have to say even more so. Her ideas were so beyond anything anyone had ever come up with or had even thought of still today. If only she had done more experimenting. She would've discovered that the crystal essences while dormant were harmless but, once powered, they were highly unstable without causing so much death. Contained experiments are what was and still are needed.

This was something he had been trying to tell Ira all along, but Ira refused to listen. Looking at another picture that sat on his dresser, he scowled. Pam Krios, leader of the Alpha Faction and his ex, smiled back at him. She sided with Ira against him and told him that if he ever wanted to get anywhere he should just conform to the regiment.

She didn't appreciate when he told her that unlike her, he wasn't willing to become someone's lap dog. Maybe it was harsh, but she called all his ideas nonsense and implied that he was only doing this to clear his ancestor's name. Yeah, he wanted to clear her name, but he wouldn't do it without having solid proof and as his girlfriend she should have supported him.

He knew it bothered her when he called her Alpha Leader; he hated it as well, not that he would ever admit to it, but it was his self-preservation. As long as he called her Alpha Leader and not her name, he could remember exactly who she was. She was the Alpha Leader, not his Pam any longer.

With a sigh, he closed his eyes. That was all ancient history as far as he was concerned. Pam was Ira's pet, and he refused to be anyone's pet. He wasn't sure why he still kept her picture. He should just toss it in the garbage where it belongs. He really should.

If only he could prove everyone wrong.

*****

"Got another load for ya Claw, bud."

Claw nodded to Roy, who was pushing in the mining cart full of crystals through the Gamma's headquarters. There was a railway track from the mines that ran right into their headquarters and through the main area in the center where his faction could process the crystals. It was very efficient, and the Gamma got along with the gnomes of Sanctuary, so it was a good working relationship.

The Gamma faction was called the Crystal Keepers of Sanctuary. Well, that was the nice term that was used to describe them. They knew all things crystal and could tell a dud by just holding it in the palm of their hands. They were the ones who decided if a crystal would be good for offense, defense, or would be productive.

Offense crystals were used by the Command Center fighters: usually those in any of the factions, although many of the other workers around the Command Center had been trained to use Crims, the crystal weapons that the Gamma's created in their fight against the shadows. Crims weren't as rare as you would think. They have many Crims that were sitting in storage unused. The reason is that not just anyone can use a Crim. A Crim calls to its wielder. If there is no connection between the two then a Crim is nothing more than a flashlight, a highly dangerous flashlight, but still a flashlight.

The light from the Crims is what they use to drive the shadows back; shadows can't stand the light. It hurts them. The greater the light, the more power to drive the shadows back and possibly even defeat it completely.

They have other weapons they have created with the crystals, with much protesting from Ira. Lucius is the only reason they have been able to utilize them. However, very few of the factions will use them because of the fact that Ira doesn't endorse them. They are crystal grenades that explode on impact, a light thrower that works pretty much like a flame thrower just to name a few, and the Gammas are always working on new ideas to help in the shadow battle.

Defense Crims were the ones used by the healers. They consist of mainly the healing crystals to heal wounds, especially those inflicted on the normies. Normies is Claw's definition of those who live outside Sanctuary and know nothing of the shadows or mythics that live there. Also, there were illusion crystals the healers used to contain the knowledge of shadows and Sanctuary from the normies along with memory Crims to adjust the memory of any normie that happened to get a first-hand glimpse of their world. Those were the main defense weapons, but there were more as well.

He didn't have much time for the healers. In his opinion, they had sticks shoved so far up their arses that it would take a surgical team to remove them all.

Productive Crims were the ones used by the maintenance workers around Sanctuary. They kept the power running and instruments working. Doors, lights, cleaning: you name it, and they did it.

Today, Claw had more on his mind now than the other workers at Sanctuary. Right now, he was looking over a crystal that his second, Tanner, was showing him. In the center of the crystal, it looked like another crystal was forming. Claw had to agree with Tanner that it did, indeed, look like that, but he knew better. The vibes he was getting from this crystal meant that there was crystal essence inside, and that essence was powered up like a gnome on a Saturday night.

The crystal was doing a good job of containing that essence, and that was why Tanner, who was almost as good as Claw when it came to crystals, couldn't feel the power. But Claw was the best when it came to crystals, and he knew that what he was holding was a time bomb. A time bomb he wanted to learn how to control - in a controlled setting, of course.

"Process the crystals Tanner. I need to take a closer look at this crystal." He wanted to get it into one of the containment rooms upstairs and see if there was anything special about this crystal that allowed it to contain such powered essence without it leaking out.

Tanner nodded to him and went to help Roy as Claw walked away staring down into the depths of the crystal, oblivious to anything but the crystal that was in his hands. With each step he took, he could feel his excitement rise.

"Watch out! Fritz alert!"

Claw tried to move out of the way, but it was too late. Fritz, the crazy red-haired sprite, had zoomed into the Gamma quarters in his little race car that Tobias had made him and zig-zagged around the warehouse in between the legs of the Gamma workers, causing them to lose balance. Claw never minded him before, but that was because Fritz never messed with him.

Jules, one of his people, had managed to save some newly-created Crims from toppling to the floor from the table where they sat rather peacefully in a tote waiting for transport. In doing so, she sent a nearby chair flying against the back of Claw's knees, which sent him falling down and the crystal that he was holding to fly across the room.

"Nawwwwww."

They all watched as if in slow motion as the crystal flew against the far wall in their quarters, and everything exploded. Claw had to cover his face with his arms to protect him from the flying debris. He stared at the hole in the back wall to his warehouse. The hole that now symbolized all his hopes of moments ago: gone up in smoke.

Claw turned and glared at Fritz who was staring at the hole in the wall with wide eyes. When Claw managed to push himself from the floor, Fritz realized he had worn out his welcome. With a squeal of tires, he was gone. That was a good thing because if Claw had managed to get his hands on him, he would have strangled the little troublemaker.

"Claw, you okay?" Tanner had come running up to him. "Looks like we don't need any tests run on the crystal now.

The only question I have is how did energized essence get inside that crystal?"

"Or why you weren't able to tell it?" Jazmine shook her head at them both, her dark eyes staring at Claw, making him a bit uncomfortable. Jazmine was the only one of his team that wasn't nervous around him and didn't care to call him out when she felt he was overstepping, which was often.

Claw breathed in, trying to keep his anger at bay. He had known it was crystal essence, and he was sure Jazmine knew that, although he wouldn't admit to that, not even to his own team. It wasn't that he didn't trust them; there wasn't a one on his team that he didn't trust. He just didn't want to pull them into this without proof. His Gamma faction would follow wherever he would lead them, but he never wanted to lead them into trouble unless he was sure it would end well.

He glared at the debris as the maintenance workers started to clean up the mess; there was no way he would be able to get any of the crystal for testing. They would be taking everything they found right to Ira.

"Everyone take the rest of the day off," Claw growled very loudly. "It will take them all day tae clean up this mess anyways."

"What about the shipment that Pam has been waiting on?" Jules pointed to the tote she had managed to save. The Crims looked fine, but there was debris all over them, and that meant that they needed to be cleaned. Well, not really, but Claw couldn't refuse the chance to put a wrench in the Alpha Leader's plans.

"They will need tae clean up the mess and those Crims as well." Claw shrugged. "Blame it on the bampot who let the wee sprite in. Canna do a thing about it."

He turned and stalked out of the Gamma quarters without another word. Pam could wait till her precious Ira cleared the area. See how she felt about him then.

He was so irate, he didn't even grin at all those who hurried to get out of his way. His jaw was clenched. The story about what had happened had probably already been told to over half of the Command Center, so they could assume he was angry about the damage all they wanted. They didn't need to know the truth, that he was more upset about the fact that possibly having the answer to controlling energized essence had been literally flung from his hands.

Till that little sprite had to wreck it. If he didn't know better, he would have sworn that the little fink worked for Ira. But there wasn't a mythic that had any loyalty to Ira, mainly because he always turned down any mythic that wanted to work in the Command Center. He hated it that gnomes controlled the crystal mines and if not for Lucius, he would have had that overturned long ago.

Only one known crystal essence weapon existed: the Rotary. And there was no one who could control it. He had petitioned to be able to examine the Rotary, but Ira denied him every time. Lucius was for it, but the Leaders sided with Ira. Consequently, he didn't know if it was the same Mythirian Metal that was used with the Crims containing the essence or if it was some special type of crystal substance.

All because some eejit had to try to grab it without any testing and lost their hand. One reason he stayed away from the Crim room was that the Rotary sat on a table in there floating between four containment rods that kept it from doing any more damage.

Thanks to Ira, he would never know what makes the Rotary work. He would never know if there is any way to mimic it and possibly defeat the shadows without having to depend on the fictional Guardians that everyone has been anxiously waiting for.

Well, not everyone. That thought made him chuckle. The Alpha Leader wasn't anxiously waiting them. He knew for a fact that deep down, she was hoping they wouldn't arrive during her time as Alpha Leader. She never told him why, but he was sure it was because she liked being the top dog and, according to history, from the moment the Guardians arrive at Sanctuary, they will run the whole Sanctuary and everything will revolve around them. That is, until they go off to fight the Magine and then never return.

Then the cycle will repeat itself, and Sanctuary will wait the arrival of the new Guardians. He thought it stupid himself. They call him insane but according to some prophet or whatever the definition of insanity is doing the same thing over and over again expecting different results.

He looked up at the sky as he thought that he wasn't sure that the powers that be expected different results. He and some others felt that they expected exactly the same results, and that was what they wanted.

Shaking his head, he pushed those thoughts out of it. He knew the dangers of those thoughts. He just hoped the Guardians did arrive during Pam's time as Alpha Leader and that he was still around to watch the show. Of course if Ira had his way, he would be long gone.

******

Sitting at the Czaar's Cantina with Gage, Claw could feel the stress start to slowly dissipate. They were watching a couple satyrs playing Rainbow Ball and laughing every time a ball went flying to the other side of the room. After the third time, the gnomes sitting at the table had had enough and rose. The satyrs scattered out the nearest exit, and the whole Cantina erupted in laughter.

"So, I hear there was another accident in Gamma quarters earlier today?"

Claw took a sip of his fruity brew of Silest's before answering Gage. If it were anyone else, he would have knocked them off their chair, but Gage he admired. Gage had his own story that no one knew, not even Claw, and he was usually able to glean any story he wanted. Gage was the calming force behind the Alpha faction. With a leader as hot tempered as Pam, it was needed. He used to enjoy when she got all riled up. Used to.

Gage was always able to diffuse the situation, but he had his own hardness about him that no one ever seemed to notice. Maybe because he always hid it behind that carefree grin of his. Pam once told him that she thought Gage would make a better

Alpha Leader, but he didn't want the position. Gage was content being her second in command, something Claw never understood; but, then again, Claw liked being in command.

"There is always an accident in the Gamma's quarters. We create and test the Crims along with other nasties." Claw kept his answer purposely vague. Gage was another that had tried to back Claw about the crystal essence, saying that it was something that should be studied rather than ignored. So much power and everyone would rather rely on some fictional Guardians than take the chance on something they could actually hold in their own hands.

Gage gave a solemn nod. "Pam was worried when she heard the news."

"I'm sure she was, but she will get her precious Crims when the maintenance crew cleans it all up," Claw practically grunted back at him.

"Yeah, I'm sure that's what she was thinking." Gage just shook his head. He opened his mouth to say something but must have thought better of it and closed it again. Tossing some coins on the table, he nodded to Claw. "If you need some help in the clean-up, we are a bit slow right now."

Claw nodded back to him then watched as he walked out of the Cantina with a nymph watching him leave. Gina. Poor thing had the worst crush on Gage, but he couldn't return her feelings. To him, she was like a little sister, something she hated hearing and got him tied to the elder tree long ago.

"Claw," a hesitant voice from behind sounded, and he turned to see Lily, a small brunette who worked with administration in the Command Center. He raised a brow at her waiting for her to tell him why she was standing in front of him wringing her hands together as if standing in front of a teacher preparing to give a half-hearted excuse for not finishing last night's homework. He wanted to tell her that he wouldn't make a good professor but refrained from doing so. "You have a call from Alaska waiting for you in the Command Center."

"Does Ira know about it?"

Lily gave a tentative smile and shook her head.

Good.

Alaska? What could Cecil want? He knew it was him because he was the only one who ever contacted Claw from there. Even when he was wanted by another from there, it was Cecil who called him. He nodded to Lily and rose from the table, drank back the rest of his fruity brew, and tossed a few of his own coins on the table. Winking at Lily, he walked past her and headed towards the Command Center. Time to see what Cecil had for him. After this morning, he could use some good news.

******

"Yer sure?" Claw was practically climbing through the view screen wanting to get to the Alaskan Sanctuary but trying to look and act calm.

"Yes, the merpeople have found some interesting crystals in the mines along the Sound floor. Kayne has asked for your input on it if you're able break away for a bit."

There was nothing out of the ordinary with this request. Cecil and other Gamma Leaders from other Sanctuaries have made similar requests to him during his time as Gamma Leader. He doubted there was a Sanctuary he hadn't seen. But it was the gleam in Cecil's eye that told Claw there was more to this request.

"There was a wee 'accident' in the Gamma quarters earlier that they're still cleaning up; looks like I've plenty of time on me hands." Claw grinned.

"Good. Kayne is talking with Ira now, so you better start packing." Cecil grinned. There wasn't an Arion in any Sanctuary that didn't know how Ira felt about Claw. If he could, Ira would kick Claw out of Sanctuary completely. Loud voices from Ira's office told him that Kayne was informing Ira right now that he needed Claw in Alaska.

"Gimme five minutes." Claw grinned, cutting the feed and walking towards his personal quarters to pack. Today was starting to look up.

******

Walking through the halls of the Alaskan Sanctuary Command Center and heading to the lowest levels where the Gamma faction headquarters was located, Claw grinned at the mermaids that were swimming through the walls of Sanctuary. Unlike the Command Center back home, this one welcomed the Mythics into their society, and everyone interacted with them on the islands around the Sound.

The Alaskan Sanctuary was located beneath the waters of the Prince William Sound, and it encompassed much of the sound floor. How much he didn't know, but he knew the Sanctuary was extensive. The walls were actually glass with the water and sea life from the Sound able to swim through. There were many spots where the walls only went about six feet or so high, so that the merpeople could visit with the Alaskan Arions.

The crystals here in Alaska were mined by the merpeople who had access to the Command Center just like any other Arion worker. Ira could learn so much from Kayne. He had thought many times about being transferred to this Sanctuary, but he wasn't about to let himself get demoted. With Cecil being Gamma Leader here that is what would happen. Although Kayne did tell him that if Ira managed to get him kicked out, he would take him in. Kayne didn't much care for Ira's management skills any more than the rest of them.

The mermaids here in Alaska weren't like the mermaids back home that swam in the lake outside the home of the Guardians, although he considered it more Lucius' home than theirs. The mermaids back home had regular looking skin that was white, pink, or bronze. Here in Alaska, all mermaids' skins had a blue, purple, or even green hue. It was said around the Command Center here that it was because of how cold the water was in the sound. After all, he had heard MANY times over how if a person were to accidentally fall into the water here, hypothermia would kill them in fifteen minutes. The same is said because they have two sets of eye lids: one that blinks like normal and a set that will blink side to side.

They were very intimidating looking creatures, deadly but beautiful looking. That could be why he found them so interesting, almost like a kindred spirit he grinned.

"Hi Claw."

Turning, he saw Jess standing there twirling a brown lock of hair around her finger. There was a flannel shirt tied at her waist. She had on jean shorts and those rubber boots the Alaskans love to wear. It was well-known that she liked him; Cecil told him many times.

"Jess, how ye doing lass?" His Scottish accent was thick as he smiled at her. He liked her, just not in the way she wanted him to, and he refused to lead her on. She was lovely and sweet, just not his type.

When she didn't answer but smiled shyly, he walked past her with a nod and started down the corridor leading down to the Gamma quarters. As he descended, the hallway got darker with eerie lights floating through the waters around him, helping to light his way. The Gamma quarters here were avoided just like his but for a different reason: not many liked walking through these hallways. Too eerie they said. Claw actually found it comforting.

As he reached the end of the hallway, he grinned when the wall parted to give him entry into Cecil's domain. The loud bass and keyboard tones were blaring at him along with a very high octave voice that was singing.

"Claw!" Cecil looked up from the dark blue crystals at which he was looking. His magnifier glasses were on, making him look like a human bug. Claw was glad he never needed them; he could tell anything he needed about crystals by just holding them in his hands.

Clasping Cecil on his shoulder, his very bony shoulder, Claw grinned at him. "It's been too long. Not sure how ye heard me enter with that loud noise blaring all around us."

"Don't start that again." Cecil shrugged off his hand in irritation then jumped up from his chair in excitement. Cecil was the only one Claw knew who could go from irritated to excited in less than a turn of a crystal.

Cecil waved his hand, and the music lowered to a decimal that wasn't trying to blast out Claw's eardrums. Claw had nothing against music but mostly he liked the classical tunes Serdita would play back home, not this bumping and grinding music that Cecil liked.

"You really need to expand your library and tastes man. Circe has the voice of a siren." Cecil grinned.

Claw raised a bushy red brow. "Ye do read yer Greek Mythology right?"

Cecil laughed. "Of course I do and if you saw Circe live, you wouldn't mind being turned into a pig by her."

"I think yer psych evaluation is overdue." Claw's eyes crinkled in laughter at the gesture Cecil sent his way. "Ye touch yer mother with that hand?" A roll of Cecil's eyes, and Claw had to concede that he had enough fun at his expense. "So, gonna tae tell me about this great discovery ye had tae show me?"

This had Cecil grinning broadly with a glint of mischief in his eyes. This had to be good.

"Come this way." He motioned for Claw to follow him further into the room past other Gamma workers and merpeople who were delivering the crystals they had mined in miner carts that were made of seaweed and sediment from the sound floor.

Once, long ago, Claw had joked about them using seashells for carts like normal mermaids. It took him all day to dry out. Some merpeople had no sense of humor.

They entered a room off the back that Claw couldn't remember ever being there before but then again, there were a lot of secret rooms in this place just like there was at home. Tables lined around the room, but only the ones along the back wall had anything on them. There were a handful of funny looking shells scattered across the top.

"What are those?"

"You tell me. They aren't crystals."

"Ye think?" Claw snorted derisively, staring at the shells curiously. Cecil just ignored that. "Tell me this isnae yer big news." If it was, Cecil was sleeping on the sound floor tonight. "They resemble the walls of the buildings in the mermaid colony."

Cecil just grinned. "Move closer," he said, lifting his chin towards the table. Claw trusted Cecil with his life, but he wasn't sure how he felt about that grin.

"It won't bite, I promise." Cecil chuckled when Claw didn't move but continued to stare at the shells. "Not in the mood to sleep on the Sound floor."

That stopped Claw. Either Cecil had the ability to read minds or he was becoming too predictable. Neither option settled with Claw very well.

In for a penny.

With a narrowed look at Cecil, he moved closer to the back table but stopped before he reached it. He could feel the energy radiating from the shells. He turned around with a wide-eyed look at Cecil who was nodding with a grin.

"Essence?"

Cecil continued to nod, his grin growing with each nod. Soon enough, he would be one big grin. He looked down and was amazed at what he saw: blue shells with energized essence residing in the aperture where once a living organism had lived.

What was really amazing was that the essence was still energized. Usually once energized, essence touched the air and it either exploded or became diluted. It was for that reason alone that the leaders sided with Ira against him doing testing on it, deeming the chances too great for injuries.

"Where was this found?"

"Laz found it while mining in the water caves."

He could hear the excitement in Cecil's voice as he spoke of one of the mermaid miners, one that was known to hang out in the Gamma quarters. Heck, he was starting to feel it as well. This could be the break they were looking for. He didn't know how the shells were doing this, but it warranted investigation.

"Who else knows?"

"Only ones that need to know," Cecil shrugged.

This meant the ones that agreed with them and had been working behind the backs of the Leaders that had agreed with Ira that crystal essence was better left alone, mainly most of Alaskan Sanctuary and probably some friends from the other Sanctuaries around the world.

Kayne didn't micromanage the Command Center here in Alaska, saying he believed they worked better when they were given the freedom to do what they were trained to do. That didn't mean he didn't keep an eye and still run things, but he didn't try to control every aspect of the Command Center. Every head of Sanctuary was different; he personally liked Kayne the best.

"What happens when the essence is removed from the shells?"

Cecil sighed. "Diluted. We lost a whole batch testing to see if we can remove the essence and still keep its powers."

"Damn." Claw's mind was already working on a way to keep the essence from becoming diluted and no good to them when he saw the twinkle in his friend's eyes. His eyes narrowed on him. "Ye got something up yer sleeve."

The smile that spread across Cecil's face had Claw grinning as well.

"You think I would have you come all this way if I hadn't already had an idea?"

Claw punched his shoulder then chuckled at Cecil's "OW!"

"Next time lead with that ye glaikit."

"Not even going to ask what that means," Cecil chuckled. "Come on! Everyone is getting things set up as we speak."

"Everyone?"

Cecil grinned. "You will see."

Claw followed Cecil after a moment's hesitation.

"If I don't like this, yer arse is gonna be on the ground."

Cecil chuckled. "Keep your threats for after we unveil our plan. If you don't like it, then you can swing a home run if you like, but I am betting you will like it."

"Ye better hope so."

"Now I see why you are so popular," Cecil chuckled, but his gait sped up.

*****

Alaska was a beautiful island, state, or whatever they wanted to call it. It was beautiful, and Claw wasn't one to be "politically correct" about anything. The air smelled cleaner, and everywhere he looked there were mountains. Right now, he was walking around with a T-shirt and jeans, but he had also been here when there was snow on the ground, and he actually had to wear a jacket with boots.

He would rather have a winter here in Alaska than in the northern states in the lower 48, as the Alaskans called the United States. Alaskans have a language all their own, but he didn't care to learn most of it. All he cared about were his crystals, and they didn't require him to learn a whole new language.

They say the winters here are dry winters, just like the heat in Arizona is a dry heat. He always scoffed at that till the time he was in Arizona and then headed back east. He got off the plane, and he understood what dry heat meant. His clothes instantly stuck to him. Dry winter is basically the same thing, with not as much dampness.

They were riding four wheelers down the roads, along the side on the dirt trails and then down the trails away from the roads. He didn't know where they were or where they were going, but he didn't care. He loved riding the four wheelers and seeing all the mountains around him; it was an experience he thought everyone should get to do.

They were riding along the trails and roads and winding around hills and mountains. The view was spectacular. Cecil pulled off to the side of one of the roads where there was a dirt pull off. A few tourists were there snapping pictures.

The tourists were staring at them with open-mouthed expressions. Cecil with his dark looks and the others who looked like Alaskans probably was nothing to them. But to see a Scotsman with bright, red, spiky hair, white as a ghost skin, and wearing jeans with chains for a belt and black leather boots probably wasn't an everyday thing. He tipped an imaginary hat to them, and they quickly looked away.

"You love making others uncomfortable, don't you?" Jeff, a Gamma soldier, asked. Claw knew Jeff and knew he liked coming off as a cocky, smart-mouthed, know-it-all. Claw knew how to handle him, just like all the others who thought to mess with him.

Claw just stared at him, not saying a word. He could hear Cecil shake his head. Those marbles make a lot of noise. His thoughts made him smile inside but not on the outside as he continued to stare at Jeff who finally looked away and started messing with the pack on the back of his four wheeler.

"Sure do." Claw grinned.

"Enough," Cecil broke in before Jeff could come back with something else. "Let's grab a bite before we get back on the road." Cecil looked out over the mountains and gave a solemn nod before turning to grab the sandwich that Lee, his second, had handed him.

Claw looked to see what Cecil nodded to but only saw another mountain.

"The Sleeping Lady." Jess had joined him, handing him a sandwich which he took with a grin. When they had headed towards the tubes to head to the mainland, Jess had been there waiting. She was going with them.

"The Sleeping Lady?" He frowned, taking a bite out of the sandwich. They always made awesome food here, but he knew better than to ask what was in it. Better to not know and just enjoy it.

"That is who Cecil was paying homage to."

He frowned at her and looked back, still seeing nothing but a mountain.

Jess moved closer and pointed to the mountain that he saw in the distance in the middle of the water.

"If you look closely, that mountain out there is in the shape of a sleeping lady.

You can see her figure and her head." Jess moved her hand to emphasize what she was saying. Claw still didn't see it but nodded anyways. "You should read up on that legend; it is a heartbreaking one."

"Why would I wanna read up on something depressing?" He frowned.

"Why read up on Greek Mythology?" Cecil countered, leaning against his vehicle.

Claw shrugged. "Cause we live it daily."

Cecil raised a dark brow at him.

"Ye tell me when I will need tae ken about some mountain that resembles a sleeping lass."

Claw finished his sandwich and wadded the bag up in his hand. Jess grabbed it before he could toss it and put it in her bag on her four wheeler to dispose of later.

"You never know." Cecil jumped back on his four wheeler. "Okay guys, saddle up, shut up, and let's ride."

Cecil really was living in the wrong state; he needed to live out west. Claw shook his head and jumped on his own machine and, with a flick of his wrist, they were off.

Following the road around a bend, he saw some buildings in the distance. Cecil pulled into a parking lot and parked his four wheeler next to a van with a stick figure family. Claw chuckled when he saw a brown pixie-haired Arion drawing a dragon eating one of the figures. He hated those stupid things, but that wee pixie had potential.

"Another folklore tae pay homage tae?" Claw looked at Cecil, who was not getting off his machine.

Cecil shook his head and unlatched the bags from his machine, tossing them over his shoulder. The others followed suit.

He frowned as he saw a sign that read "Independence Mine." What were they doing at a tourist attraction? They were supposed to be working on experimenting with crystal essence.

"I ken Alaskans do it differently but tae do Sanctuary work in front of normies?"

Lee frowned at him. "Normies?"

"Let it go, Lee," Cecil told her, but Claw could see she didn't appreciate his nickname for the regular people. Too many bleeding hearts everywhere he went.

"Just wait, Irish."

Now he knew he had gotten on Cecil's nerves; he only called him Irish when he was irritated with him. There were some Scotsmen who didn't care about being called Irish and then there was Claw. You didn't call him Irish, not unless you planned to take a nice long flight across the room that is. Knowing he deserved it for his words, he let it slide. If any of the others decided to get froggy about it, though, there was no promises.

But none did; they were too busy unloading all their supplies as if the whole area wasn't full of tourists. He was amazed at how many Arions had joined them, that and the fact that they were all from the different factions.

"Man, Ira could really learn something from Kayne."

"What?" Lee jerked around, but he just shook his head and grabbed a piece of jerky from his satchel, chewing on it while he watched. He still wasn't sure what was up Cecil's sleeve, but he couldn't wait to see what the beanpole, and he meant that fondly, was up to.

There was a big grey and red building that was towering over all the other buildings close to the parking lot.

"That was where the single miners lived."

Turning around, he saw the same pixie-haired girl who had drawn the dragon on the back windshield of the van staring at him, twirling a silver instrument between her fingers that he knew was for working with crystals.

"Miners?"

"This is the Independence Mine State Park," she told him with a nod as she tossed a bag to a boy that was almost skinnier than Cecil. "They call it a ghost town."

He raised a brow at that. "Are there really ghosts here?"

"Awww is the great Scots afraid of Casper? Don't worry; we won't let the Tommyknockers get ya," Dale, one of the

Alpha soldiers, grinned before disappearing up the walkway before Claw could respond. Lee just smiled but said nothing.

The girl just continued as if Dale hadn't spoken. She didn't even look like she had even heard what he said. "There is when we want them to be." That was said with a mischievous grin. Patches was her name, and she was called Patches of all trades, mainly because she could fix anything, crystal or not.

She worked with Cecil because of her affinity with crystals but was known to work with all factions in Alaska if needed. Something Ira should really take notes on. Oh, who was he kidding? There was a lot Ira should be taking notes on. Her pixie hair was brown, and her eyes were as bright as the Alaskan sky above them. And since it was June that meant they were very bright.

Wow, did he really just think that? Since when did he become a poet?

Patches was a cute wee thing with a flannel shirt, jean shorts, a leather tool belt that was always around her waist as a fashion accessory, and work boots. Why couldn't he have fallen for her instead of Pam? She was more his type; they both loved working with crystals and didn't care what others thought of them. Maybe when this was all said and done he might see about coming back and watching the Northern Lights with her.

"Pay attention or you will miss it." Lee nudged him, jerking him out of his daydreams and causing Cecil to snicker.

"I'm thinking he was paying attention to something more interesting."

The gesture he gave Cecil wasn't very nice, but Lee and Patches were too busy watching the paved walkways to notice. Thank Zeus.

A shout caught his attention as several guys came running down the pathway screaming in their white slacks, white cloth shoes, and collared fancy shirts.

"Ghost! Ghost!"

They couldn't get to their cars quick enough, and they could hear them peeling out in their haste with others following frantically behind them.

"Momma!" A little girl had fallen in the rush, but Lee jumped on a nearby boulder and leaped over the crowd, grabbing the child and returning her to her very thankful mother.

He and Cecil watched as the rest of the tourists climbed hastily into their vehicles and got out of there as fast as their wheels could take them.

"So what do ye do when ye find someone who isnae scared of ghosts?"

Cecil shrugged and gave a wicked grin. "That is when we get inventive."

"And have fun," Patches smirked as she started up the hill after Lee.

Yeah, he was sure he could have fun with her.

They started up the paved walkway behind Lee who was almost to the tall grey and red building, where there looked to be several transparent apparitions standing on the porch. One was a very rotund looking miner that reminded him of some movie he had seen several years ago.

Looking around, he noticed that Patches had disappeared.

"Loose something? Or should I say someone?"

He ignored the smirking Cecil. As they got closer, the apparitions started to disappear, and there stood a couple of grinning Arions.

He gave a nod and looked around. "So exactly what are we doing here?"

Cecil pointed to one of the buildings that looked as if one good gust of wind would knock it over. "That is where we are going to set up our first experiment. That building will work as a cage as soon as we can get a shadow inside."

"If it doesn't fall in on us," Claw grunted.

"Where is your sense of adventure?" Lee smirked at him before walking right past him and towards the pile of lumber where Patches was already barking out orders to others who were working around the exterior of the building, crystals in hand.

*****

Inside the building, there were even more Arions setting things up. Crystals were being strategically placed to make sure the building remained standing. He looked around for the shells but couldn't see them. Exactly how were they going to be testing the essence if it wasn't here?

Claw leaned against a wall with his arms crossed, watching as the others pulled out more crystals and then suited up as if readying for a shadow battle. They grabbed their Crims and started to the door. Lee turned to look at him.

"Are you coming or would you rather wait here while we do all the footwork?"

That lass had a mouth on her; he liked it. His lips turned up in a grin. He was never one to turn down a challenge as he pushed away from the wall and followed them out of the building. Maybe transferring to Alaska wouldn't be so bad. He could let Cecil keep the leader position and he could just work with his crystals.

"So, what are we doing?"

"We need test subjects, right?"

"Ay." He nodded in agreement with Cecil who grinned and kept walking. Turning around, he saw Patches working with others mounting the blue shells all around the outside perimeter of the roof. He could see the shield crystals that were placed strategically beneath them as well. "What are they doing?" He was afraid he knew. He had no problem with this if it was just him and Cecil, but adding all the others?

"We need cages, right?" Casey, one of the Theta's who was popping her gum and twirling her Crim around in her hand, asked. He was surprised a Theta was actually able to find time to partake in this excursion. Thetas in Alaska were like the Alphas back home. Just like back home, they were considered the hunters and trackers. However, here in Alaska that was more revered than just being a leader, which showed how the whole Sanctuary here viewed this experiment.

"The shack with the crystal essence holders you are looking at is the cage," Lee told him. He frowned. She rolled her eyes at him. "We get a shadow to follow us and lead them into the shack. The healers will release the shield crystals causing the holders to topple over with the essence, creating essence blankets all around."

"Essence containment," Cecil grinned.

Claw wasn't grinning. He was looking at his good friend as if he had lost his mind.

"But once the essence leaves the shells it will just become diluted."

"Not if it falls through a magically charged filter placed along the exterior just under the shells and soaks up the power."

And everyone back home called him a loon.

"That much charged essence? We dinnae ken how it will react. It could blow that shack back tae the lower 48 as ye say."

"Come on, Claw. I thought you were one who liked to live dangerously."

"Dangerously and suicidal are two different things." Claw glared at Cecil. "If it was just us than fine but this is putting others at risk as well. I will nea put others at risk."

"Don't you think that is our choice to make?" Lee glared at him, but he ignored her.

"Cecil-"

"Look, Claw. They wanted in and are willing to take the risks here. If this works out the way I think it will, everyone here will make Sanctuary history. You can't expect them to not want to be part of this just because your Head of Defense is a mamby pamby."

"Besides, Patches is here running containment crystal procedures in case our testing doesn't work out like we plan," Lee interjected. "And no one knows crystals like our Patches."

Claw raised a brow over that one, but Lee wasn't backing down; her hands on her hips showed him that.

"Fine, but why nae at least test the essence before bringing in a shadow?"

Claw didn't mind putting himself in danger; Cecil was Gamma leader as well and understood the consequences. The others, though, all they could see is the chance at making history.

"Because those were the only shells that we were able to smuggle out." Cecil looked a bit abashed, and Claw wasn't sure if he was furious or confused.

"Smuggled out?" he asked very slowly.

"As you said, they look like the same material used on the merpeople's homes."

Oh, Claw wasn't sure he liked where this was going.

"The merpeople are very protective of it."

Claw's eyes narrowed on his good friend. "Ye said Laz gave ye those shells."

Cecil looked a bit uncomfortable. "Maybe 'gave' isn't the right word." When Claw took a step forward, Cecil continued. "What could I do man? It was essence; the merpeople don't even know what it is. They wouldn't miss it. When Laz brought in a crystal delivery, I saw the shells sitting there in a cart that he was taking back to the palace." His one shoulder shrugged. "I scammed it when Laz was too busy flirting with Jaz."

Now Claw understood. This was their only chance to see if they could actually get the essence to work for them. Didn't mean he had to like it. Claw nodded then moved forward and swung, his fist catching Cecil in the jaw and sending him landing on his butt on the rocky ground. The others ran up quickly, but Cecil just held up his hand to stop them while rubbing his jaw with his other hand.

"I deserved that, but you only get one," he told Claw, and Claw nodded back at him. Cecil knew how he hated being kept in the dark and having surprises sprung on him like this, even if he had no problem doing it to others.

Claw looked around at the others, who were watching him and looking a bit nervous.

"Ye all do this, and it is on yer own shoulders."

With that said, he turned and looked at Cecil who was now standing. He practically growled, "Well, what are ye waiting for? Let's do this."

****

They hadn't walked far when they saw a Shadow creature ambling around the mountainside, close to the state park. Claw watched as the Shadow shifted through wooden planks in the river up the mountain, as if it was looking for something. It wasn't one of the big Shadow creatures; this one looked like one of the small minions.

"They are attracted to this area cause of the Tommyknockers," Lee told him aiming her crossbow Crim at the Shadow. She pulled back on the string, and a bright arrow of light appeared.

"Tommyknockers?" This was the second time he had heard that term today.

"That is what they call ghosts that were killed in the mines," Cecil explained as his Crim turned into a pair of light crystal blades that arced over his knuckles as if they were a pair of brass knuckles, brass knuckles that could slice and dice a Shadow that got too close.

"Get ready, boys. We need to herd this little minion to the cage," Lee was telling them as she pulled back on the crossbow and let the arrow fly.

"No!"

Claw jerked at Cecil's exclamation and saw the arrow hit a rock right by the minion, lighting up the whole area as other screams could be heard. There wasn't just one minion there; there were many and not all small and munchkin looking either. They were in trouble.

"You boys wanted to test out that containment idea; let's hope that it can contain more than just one," Lee said, already arming her crossbow with another arrow as Claw pulled out his Crim and started twirling it in his hand as his battle axe took form.

"Let's see if we can lessen the numbers before we try it," Claw grunted as he twirled around and brought the axe down on the head of a Shadow that had advanced on him. He watched as Jeff started twirling something around his head that had crystal balls on the end. He let it fly, and it wrapped around a Shadow several times before the crystal balls smacked it in the midsection. The Shadow screamed and crawled to a shadow on the ground to escape.

He almost shouted to Jeff, worried the guy was going to lose his Crim but as he watched, the bola unattached itself and flew back to Jeff, better than a boomerang.

A few others joined in with their Crims glowing and even managed to get a few Shadows down, but there were still more coming. Claw tried to stop the grin that was forming as he saw the Alaskan Alpha Leader Cameron join the fray just in time to keep a Shadow from sneaking up on Lee.

"Let's show these guys how it feels to be hunted," Lee grinned at him as she shot another arrow at two of the Shadows who were attempting to double team Casey who was twirling her Crim rope around her as a shield. They quickly turned their attention from her and back to Lee who grinned at him. "Now let's head back towards the others."

They all took off running with Shadows following them, moving through the light and using the few shadows that were being thrown by boulders and other buildings around them to travel through. How he hated when the Shadows did that. When they would disappear in one shadow, you never knew which one they would come out of. Better to fight where there were no shadows.

Cecil was tripped by a Shadow hand that reached out from a shadow being thrown by the elevated tramway above them. Claw rolled and brought his axe down on the hand. The Shadow screamed as the hand disappeared in the sunlight like a puff of smoke.

"Getting slow there," Claw grinned then ducked as a Shadow attempted to jump him from the shadows. He kept running.

"As long as our team with the essence release isn't slow," Cecil replied, arcing his arm out. The blade caught a Shadow that got too close, and the scream could be heard all around the mountains.

These Shadows were persistent when it came to something they wanted, and Arion warriors were their favorite meal besides the mythics.

Crystal light bombs were raining from above them, exploding in flashes of light and causing the Shadows to scream around them. Looking up, there was Nessie riding in the mining cart on the tramway and using a sling shot Crim. It looked so rickety, but Claw knew it was stable.

It was only unstable to normies.

They kept trying to herd the Shadows to the shack where the essence was waiting to cage them. Then, they would find a way to finally destroy the Shadows and no longer would they need to wait for the Guardians to show up.

But only if the Shadows would cooperate. Okay, even he had to chuckle at himself over that one. Since when have the bad guys in any flick or show ever cooperated? Did they really expect the Shadows to just walk into the shack and stand there, giving them the chance to trap them? It seemed that Cecil hadn't truly thought this through.

Claw looked around him at the battles going on. They had managed to get down to a handful of Shadows, but they couldn't afford to lose them or else this would've been all for nothing. They needed a plan now but what? The Shadows were trying to capture the Arions around them but not bad enough to follow any of them into the shack. They just turned and went after another Arion that was outside the shack.

"You are so ugly that you went into a haunted house and came out with an application!"

Claw stared at Jeff as he taunted the Shadows and insulted them, trying to get them to follow him. When his bolas wrapped around the neck of one and the ball smacked its head, the Shadow did turn to start after him but as soon as he ducked into the shack, it turned and went after Patches who was already battling a Shadow with her kitana Crims.

He was about to intervene when an arrow distracted the Shadow before it could do any damage. There had to be something they wanted more than the Arions. Something with more magic.

More magic!

That was it!

He pulled out the pouch from his pocket with the petals that Gina had given him earlier in the week to give to Gage. He knew better than to do that; everyone in Sanctuary knew Gina fancied Gage and that she would do anything to get him, including using nymph magic. He was going to give them to Lucius, but the discovery of the crystal entombed essence and what happened afterwards had distracted him.

He looked at the Shadows that were starting to get the upper hand and decided it was time to find out exactly what Gina had planned for poor Gage.

As soon as he opened the pouch, the Shadows froze and turned to look at him. Yeah, Gina had put a lot of magic in these petals. He tipped the pouch and started walking back, letting the petals fall to the ground as he moved back slowly. He wasn't fool enough to touch them. As each petal hit the ground, roots grew up and as a Shadow neared it, the roots would grab the Shadow.

"Go, Claw! Go!" the others were shouting encouragement, making sure to surround the Shadows to keep them from escaping. But that wasn't really needed; the Shadows paid them no attention. The magic from the petals had them all running to get the petals.

As each Shadow reached a petal, it would let out a scream as the roots would grab it in its clutches. He hoped that the roots wouldn't try to take them to Gina. He hoped that being in Alaska was too far for her power to do that. He was sure that would have even Lucius upset with him.

To his great relief, the roots just handed the Shadows off to the next set of roots like an assembly line. If this wasn't so serious, he might have chuckled, but he kept the petals falling to the ground as he kept moving towards the shack praying he didn't run out of petals.

He breathed a sigh of relief as he moved through the doorway, dumped the remainder of the petals in the middle of the shack floor, and jumped out the back window, shouting as he did.

"Now! Do it now!"

He rolled down the rocky hill, feeling the rocks bite into him. Good thing he had jeans and a leather jacket on or else he would have been torn up. He leapt to his feet as the healers and maintenance workers quickly moved to release the shields and let the shells tip.

His chest tightened as he watched the glowing essence start to dim as it spilled from the blue shells; the shells were losing their brilliance as well.

Please let this work; please let this work. Claw never thought himself a prayer till now. He prayed to all the Greek Gods and Goddesses, to the Egyptian ones that he could remember, a few Norse ones that he knew of, and even to the Christian God that most the normies he knew prayed to. He wasn't leaving anything to chance.

Hope bloomed within his chest as the essence shifted through the power charged crystal filters beneath the shells and started to glow once more. That hope grew within him as the essence glowed brighter. He watched as the essence sands started to combine together to create that blanket that Cecil had hypothesized would happen.

The whole exterior of the shack glowed with the raw energy from the crystal essence sands. Shrieks could be heard from inside the shack. It seemed the Shadows had finished their snacks of nymph-powered petals and realized they were stuck inside a light bulb. There would be so much light that there would be no shadows for them to hide in.

He just hoped with as much power as the essence was giving off there would be enough of the Shadow creatures to run tests on, although, if not, they still had enough here to force Ira to let him continue his ancestor's work.

Triumphant shouts could be heard all around the park as Arions high-fived each other, grinning like a bunch of school kids. They had accomplished something that no Arion in history had ever done, something that even the mythical Guardians had never done.

They had captured not only one but several Shadow creatures.

Claw ignored the hands that clapped his back in congratulations and the words of praise. He was still staring at the glowing building in front of them all. Could it finally be happening? After all these years and failed tests, did they finally have the means to possibly defeat the Shadows once and for all? He could clear his ancestor's name and show a certain Alpha Leader that he wasn't some crackpot, that he was someone to be admired.

That thought had him grinning as others twirled around with their hands clasped, dancing in glee. Cecil clapped his shoulder as he stood next to him with a matching grin.

"Who needs stinking Guardians? Right, mate?"

Claw nodded with a very satisfied grin. He couldn't wait to see the expression on Ira's face.

He was about to turn and join in on the celebrations when he saw it. There in the very center of the essence blanket, a spark that kept pulsing brighter and brighter.

"Naw," he breathed. "Ye cannae do this." His elated hopes started to plunge deeper with each pulse. Soon, there were other pulses joining in all over the blanket.

"Get away!" he shouted, waving his arms and pushing others away from the shack that was getting brighter. Heat was radiating from it as well. The shrieks inside became howls of pain. If they weren't Shadow creatures he would almost feel sorry for them.

"Patches!" Lee shouted, and Claw turned seeing the little impish jack of all trades staring up at the building as if in shock.

He darted towards the shack, ignoring the terrified shouts of others. His arm looped around her waist and, as if she was nothing more than a child, he picked her up and ran.

"Ya daft wee lass."

He vaulted over a boulder with her as an explosion rocked the mountain around them. The force threw him several feet as he held onto Patches, trying to keep her safe.

As his body hit the hard ground, he rolled. He found them both by a wooden bridge that extended over the water that many still tried to find gold from to this day. His body felt as if it had just went through a meat grinder.

"You wanna move? You're a bit heavy."

Patches was glaring up at him.

"Little spitfire," he chuckled and, with a pained groan, he rolled from her. He looked at the wooden pieces still raining down from the sky along with the still sparkling essences. The essences sizzled as they hit the water's surface; the ones that hit ground glowed brightly for just a second before going out.

"You okay?"

Patches' irritation changed to concern. He just sighed as he looked at all the destruction around them. They were so close. So close.

"Claw! Patches! You two all right?"

Cecil, Lee, and the others had come running up to them. Claw just nodded at them, not even looking at them. He was looking at all his dreams that were floating from the sky to the ground.

All he needed now was for Ira to show up.

※※※※※※

"What the hell were you thinking?" Kayne's normally jovial face was red with suppressed anger and worry. It hadn't taken long for word to get to him. He had the whole medical staff there going over injuries, and the maintenance crew was now working on clean up. Crystals were being used to mask the area and to make it not look as if a battle had just been waged there.

"It's obvious they weren't Kayne," a booming voice that reminded Claw of over acting could be heard. He turned and there stood a very tall and regal-looking man with a scrawny kid who could've been his mini clone standing next to him.

"Who is that?"

Cecil nudged him. "That is one of Alaska's honored chiefs."

Claw frowned. "An elf?"

The tall slender man was, indeed, an elf as was his little clone that was looking over them all with a look of disdain. Claw didn't like him already. The ears were obvious as was the pinched-faced expressions that were common among elves.

"Of course an elf," Cecil said. "Most of the Chiefs here are mythics, royalty of course. The regular populace can't see it of course."

"You mean the normies," Claw grinned, and Cecil frowned.

"I don't think now is the time for your type of humor, Claw. We are in big trouble if one of the Chiefs is here."

What could they do to him? Send him home without supper? He was sure Ira already planned on that. Hell, when he got home he might be lucky to have a faction to run. He wouldn't be surprised if Ira used this to get him booted from Sanctuary. Maybe Lucius could use a houseboy or something?

Kayne turned to look at them with a serious expression, something Claw wasn't used to seeing on the Alaskan defense leader.

"Whose grand idea was this?" He looked at Cecil, who was looking at his feet looking contrite. Claw wasn't a stranger to trouble, but Cecil had rarely been in trouble. Actually, this would be the first time. "Or do I have to ask?"

"It was my idea, Kayne," Claw spoke up before anyone could say anything. "Cecil was just trying to help me test my findings out, and the others joined to try to keep everything from blowing up." The last was said with a wry grin.

Kayne raised a disbelieving eyebrow at him. "They seem to have failed."

Claw gave a half shrug with a half grin to go along with it. "They did their best, Sir."

The mini chief snorted. "Figured it would be the Cheechako who created this mess."

Claw frowned. "Cheechako?" He didn't know what that word meant, but he was sure it was something he wouldn't like considering the mini chief's expression and tone of voice. That and the scrawny clone was looking at him like he was a bug on the ground, one the clone thought he was going to squish.

He better think again.

"It means someone who is new to Alaska," Lee interjected quickly, too quickly for Claw's liking.

The clone snorted, and Kayne's eyes narrowed. "Short version or more accurate is stupid white man."

Everyone around them froze, and Kayne looked at the Chief who was grinning along with his son.

"Leonard!"

Claw could swear Kayne was not happy, but he wasn't looking to find out; he was staring at the cocky clone who had crossed his arms and leaned back against the rail on the wooden bridge on which he was standing.

"Claw," Cecil warned him as he started towards the Chief's son.

"Just wanting tae make the lad's acquaintance," Claw assured him as he moved forward, enjoying the narrowed look he was receiving from the wee chief.

As he got closer, the mini chief stood up tensely. The other Arions rushed forward, but they weren't quick enough.

None of them were. Claw swung his arm, and his fist connected with the pup's jaw sending him backwards over the railing. He landed in the stream with a splash and an outrageous protest coming from his father.

Claw just grinned down at the kid who was staring up at him eyes wide. Claw was sure no one had ever put that kid in his place before. Something that was long overdue in Claw's eyes.

Claw's satisfaction drained away as the boy's eyes went from annoyed to blank. The kid was shining from all the essence that was in the water, the sun making it look like he was covered in glitter.

His father went to help him from the stream, but Kayne pulled him back before he could touch him, barking out to the healers to get the kid back to the Sanctuary so they could see what was going on.

"What happened to my son, Kayne?" the chief bellowed loudly. He might have been a skinny guy, but his voice echoed all around as if he was a very robust fellow.

"I don't know, Leonard, and I won't know till we get him to Sanctuary and tested," Kayne tried to calm down the Chief who then turned on Claw.

"You!" he growled, pointing right at Claw. "This is all your fault."

"Aiden egged him on and you know it, Leonard," Kayne reminded him. "If he hadn't been insulting then Claw wouldn't have reacted as he did."

Leonard turned on Kayne, his face redder than Claw's hair. He seemed to have that effect on blowhards it seemed. "My son is prince of my people; he can be insulting if he wants."

Kayne's eyes narrowed. "Being royalty is no excuse for being rude. I have told you before if your children can't be polite then they aren't welcome in Sanctuary."

"This isn't Sanctuary, Kayne, and here you don't rule anything; here I rule."

"This is Sanctuary business, Leonard, and you aren't the only chief in Alaska." Kayne reminded him that he only ruled if the others were agreeable with it.

"We will see what the others say when they discover what has happened to Aiden." Leonard huffed his chest reminding Claw of one of those tiny frogs whose belly would expand when they croaked.

"Why don't we wait and see how Aiden is before we start making threats we might regret," Kayne told him tightly.

The chief glared at Claw one last time before turning and walking away with a tiny man quickly following him. Claw could almost see the man with a cloak swirling around him as he walked away.

"You better get back to your Sanctuary, Claw." Kayne sounded regretful.

Claw sighed and nodded. He kind of figured his presence in Sanctuary would probably only make matters worse. He felt bad leaving the others to the clean-up, but it couldn't be helped.

"Give me some time to smooth things over," Kayne told him and chuckled at the look of disbelief on Claw's face. "Let's see what happens, Cecil. You will have to get with Janice regarding what was in the water and let's see if we can figure out what is going on with Aiden."

Cecil nodded as he and Claw walked away.

"You didn't have to take the blame man," he told him, but Claw just shrugged.

"Not like it isnae something that I ain't used to," Claw told him.

"It's still not right. I will set it right with him as soon as we get things cleaned up."

"Dinna," Claw told him.

"But-"

"Just let it go. As I said, this willnae be the first time I have gotten in trouble, and I doubt it will be the last."

Cecil sighed. "If you say so, man."

"I do."

"Don't mean I have to like it."

Claw just shrugged. "Dinna matter; that's the way it is."

Cecil tried talking Claw into letting him tell Kayne the truth all the way back to Sanctuary, but Claw stayed firm. When they got there, they went to the porter to take him home. Claw was amazed that everyone was there to say bye to him.

Patches walked over and kissed his cheek. "You're an idiot for taking the blame like that but thank you."

"You didn't have to," Lee told him but smiled at him gratefully.

He just shrugged feeling very uncomfortable.

"We won't forget it, man," Cameron nodded to him and clasped his hand in friendship. "If you ever need anything, we all owe you."

Claw didn't know how to respond, so he didn't. He just nodded at them all and stepped up onto the platform. He had a bad feeling this would be the last time he would see Alaska. He wasn't serious when he first thought about becoming Lucius' houseboy, but it was becoming more and more of a possibility if he wanted to actually stay in Sanctuary.

*****

He had been back home for almost a week now and still nothing from Alaska. Even weirder was nothing from Ira. He expected to be pulled into his office and given his marching papers. When he saw Ira earlier, all the man did was glare at him before turning and walking the other way. Not something he expected.

The whole of Sanctuary was a buzz about what happened in Alaska, so he knew that Ira was aware of what happened. So why wasn't he grinning as he kicked Claw out? Not that he wanted that to happen, but it was what he expected.

"People are starting to wonder if you don't have something on Ira." Gage grabbed a chair and turned it around before straddling it and grinning at Claw.

"What will ya have ssssweetnesssss?" Serdita smiled down at Gage who ordered his usual, grinning at Claw who was lifting his mug and taking a long drink before responding.

"If I did ye really think I wud tell ye?" This caused Gage to chuckle. "As it is, I am nae sure why I am nae booted out myself."

Gage nodded in thanks as Daphne brought his drink. "Everyone is also trying to figure out why someone usually as loud and brash as you is being so tight lipped about the most exciting thing to hit Sanctuary since the Grendow sisters were seen by the Harlick brothers out on a date with the two drifters."

Claw rolled his eyes on that one. The brothers had torn up the whole town, and it had taken over a month to clean up and repair. The brothers considered the sisters to be theirs and pity anyone that got in their way. Zeke was caught helping one of the sisters with her packages, and he woke up one morning completely encased in a pottery vase. They still didn't know whether it was Shirk or Tad who had done it or how they had gotten in to the Delta quarters.

"I dinna ken why they want tae know what happened; it was a failure," Claw spoke, looking into his mug. He truly didn't want to think about what happened. Even though he still felt satisfaction in hitting the pompous poor excuse of an elven prince, he had a feeling the snot-nosed brat would be exacting his pound of flesh for that disgrace.

"That isn't what I heard," Gage grinned taking a drink and looking over at the Rainbow Ball table where there were a couple of satyrs currently playing.

Claw's eyes narrowed on him. "Either spit it out or leave; I dinna care which."

Gage chuckled. "Man, you need to lighten up. No wonder no one wants to sit with ya." He held his hands up in surrender when Claw stood up. Not that he was worried that Claw would deck him. Well, not entirely, but he was just messing with his buddy. "I heard that before the essence's power became overwhelming it was working as a containment cell."

Claw nodded, not sure where his friend was going with this because whether it was working or not, it still failed and possibly cost Alaska a very important state monument.

"Seems there has been talk among some in Sanctuary about the possibility of the essence actually being used to contain and finally defeat the Shadows," Gage grinned.

Claw just snorted. "Ira will snuff that talk out."

The twinkle in Gage's eyes should have warned Claw that he had been holding back the best of his news. Even if he had been warned, he would still have been shell-shocked.

"Actually, when Pam questioned him on it, he got very evasive."

Claw coughed as his drink went down the wrong tube. "Ira's pet actually questioned him on it?"

Gage just shook his head. "You know she hates it when you call her that."

Claw just shrugged.

"You would think you two would grow up and stop fighting with each other," Gage snorted.

Claw raised a brow at him.

"Neither of you have gotten with anyone since you two broke up," Gage pointed out, but Claw just shrugged.

"She cannae find anyone that meets her standards, and no one can handle me," Claw grinned at Gage who frowned at him.

"Why can't the two of you just admit that there isn't anyone else for the two of you?"

Claw was about to tell him that he did find someone else in Alaska when someone shouting his name stopped him. He raised his hand as a courier from Sanctuary came running up.

"Call from Alaska waiting in your quarters." The boy was breathless as Claw nodded to him and stood up.

Claw looked at Gage. "Ye ken, it is times like this that make me wonder why I didnae give ye the pouch."

He walked away, leaving Gage staring at him with a very confused expression on his face. Claw was okay with letting him wonder what that meant, and he had no plans on ever telling him.

*****

Claw sat at his desk, turned on the video feed, and there was Cecil staring back at him. From the expression on Cecil's face, Claw was sure this wasn't going to be just a friendly conversation.

"Might as well give me the bad news," Claw said, leaning back in his chair.

"Sorry, man. Leonard has managed to get just enough chiefs on his side, and they said the only way they will allow Sanctuary to continue to operate in Alaska is if Kayne gave them his word that you wouldn't be allowed back in Alaska." The guilt on Cecil's face was evident.

Claw just shrugged.

"Kayne told me to tell you that he appreciated what you did. Leonard has been looking for a way to close down Sanctuary since Kayne told him that if he wanted to ever step foot in Sanctuary again then he and his children will show respect to others."

Claw wasn't surprised to hear this. Alaska was a very magical place, and the mythics there weren't contained to Sanctuary. They were actually there before

Sanctuary came to be and held very prestigious positions.

"Before you ask, no I didn't tell Kayne it wasn't all your idea. He figured that one out on his own."

Claw gave a nod. He knew Kayne was no fool. That man knew more than anyone realized.

"Kayne also told me to tell ya not to worry about Ira; he spoke to the leaders about what you did for our Sanctuary, and they agreed that your sacrifice should be praised and not punished."

Claw's eyes widened at hearing this. Cecil just grinned that impish grin of his.

"Your position in Sanctuary is very secure. Kayne has said that he can't get you back into Alaska but if you need anything else, just to let him know."

Claw chuckled. "Wish I cuda been there tae see Ira's face when he was told that."

"You aren't the only one. It just sucks you are now banned from Alaska."

Claw shrugged. "I'm sure the elven ruler's little snot-nosed brat had a hand in that."

"Actually, Aiden had nothing to do with it. Well, not directly." Cecil looked like he was trying to hide a smile.

Claw raised a brow.

"When we got him down here and got him cleansed of all the essence he…" Cecil chewed on his bottom lip as if he wasn't sure how to say it.

"Just say it." Claw hated when people beat around the proverbial bush.

"Well, he changed."

"You mean he actually became a decent being?"

"No, I mean changed." Cecil moved the camera so that it showed one of the glass walls. Out on the Sound floor was a merman picking up stones and examining them before dropping them and reaching for another. His skin was a mismatch of pale pink, deep blue, and a very loud purple. When the merman looked up at him, Claw saw the two sets of eyelids blinking at him.

"That is Aiden or Adrijan as he now insists on being called. He still believes he is royalty and has been tossed out of the castle for daring to tell the mermaid princess to bow down to him. Now he just wanders around the Sound floor gathering rocks claiming they are his jewels for his crown."

Claw was stunned.

Cecil moved the camera back. "See what I mean?"

"The essence did that?"

Cecil nodded.

Claw had no words. He had never in any wild and crazy dream believed that the essence could do such a thing. To completely change one's genetics from an elf to a merman? What else could it do?

"They have to let us continue our testing now; this changes everything." Claw was leaning forward in his seat, but Cecil was slowly shaking his head.

"Actually, the leaders say what happened to Aiden only reinforces their beliefs that the essence is to be left alone. Even the diluted essence they want to be contained and kept hidden. They also banned anyone from telling what happened to Aiden; even the mythics that know were bound to this as well."

Claw's face fell. It seemed that there was nothing he could do.

"Don't look so down, Claw," Cecil told him. "You are a hero as far as Alaska is concerned."

Claw's eyes narrowed. "Ye repeat that tae anyone and I will shove yer head in a tub of essence and see if ye grow gills."

Turning off the monitor, he left his office and decided to head to the dining hall for a bite to eat. As he left the Gamma quarters, he saw Ira in the hallway. Ira glared at him before turning and storming away. That was enough to put a smile on his face as he headed towards the dining hall. Maybe it wasn't a total loss after all.

Made in the USA
Columbia, SC
03 February 2022